THE BIONIC BUNNY SHOW

CHANNEL 7

A
MARC BROWN
LAURENE KRASNY BROWN
◆PRODUCTION◆

LITTLE, BROWN
AND COMPANY
BOSTON
TORONTO

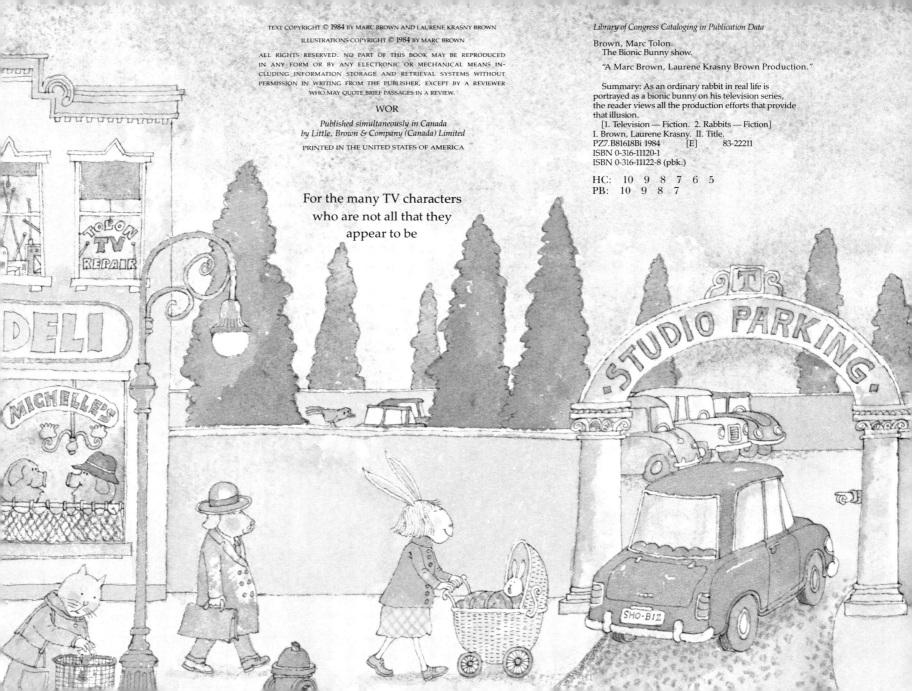

WOR

*Published simultaneously in Canada
by Little, Brown & Company (Canada) Limited*

PRINTED IN THE UNITED STATES OF AMERICA

For the many TV characters
who are not all that they
appear to be

Library of Congress Cataloging in Publication Data

Brown, Marc Tolon.
  The Bionic Bunny show.

  "A Marc Brown, Laurene Krasny Brown Production."

  Summary: As an ordinary rabbit in real life is
portrayed as a bionic bunny on his television series,
the reader views all the production efforts that provide
that illusion.
  [1. Television — Fiction. 2. Rabbits — Fiction]
I. Brown, Laurene Krasny. II. Title.
PZ7.B81618Bi 1984   [E]   83-22211
ISBN 0-316-11120-1
ISBN 0-316-11122-8 (pbk.)

HC: 10   9   8   7   6   5
PB: 10   9   8   7

"Good morning," said Wilbur.

"You're late," grumbled the director.

Wilbur had only ten minutes to get made up, go to Wardrobe, and finish learning his lines.

"Hold still," said Maxine, the makeup woman. "I have to make you look strong and smart. It isn't easy, you know!" she joked.

With practiced skill, the Wardrobe Department transformed Wilbur into the Bionic Bunny.

First they snapped on his costume with the built-in muscles.

They tied his bionic sneakers, which made him taller.

They strapped on his bionic wristwatcher, which supposedly let him see anything anywhere.

Finally, they pulled on his bionic ears, which supposedly let him hear everything.

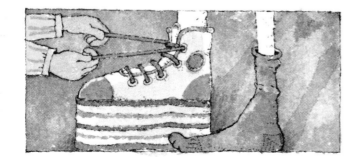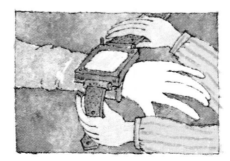

5

"Everyone on the set!" ordered the director.

"Speak up," mumbled Wilbur. "I can't hear a thing with these darn ears on."

"Move!" growled the director.

The crew switched on the lights and tested the microphones.

They moved the last sets into place, and quietly wheeled the cameras into position.

"Tilt camera one up to make Wilbur look taller in the opening shot," ordered the director. "Camera two, tilt down on the rats to make them look smaller."

"Wake up, Wilbur," called the director. "Let's make television!"

"And now," said the announcer, "the one who makes the impossible possible, the Bionic Bunny.

"With a twitch of his nose and a wiggle of his ears, he summons his bionic strength."

7

"Cut!" shouted the director. "What's the matter, Wilbur?"

"I need a Band-Aid," said Wilbur.

"If those bricks were real and not rubber you'd need more than a Band-Aid," said the cameraman.

"Now, in this next scene the robbers see you," reminded the director. "Speak loudly and look scary. Make them afraid of you!

"Places, everyone. Action!"

"Cut!" called the director. "Wilbur, you should know your lines. Sometimes it amazes me that you can even remember your name!"

The script man's voice came from the control room. "Drop those guns, you rotten robber rats!"

"Could you move the teleprompter closer?" asked Wilbur. "I can't read it without my glasses."

"So much for your bionic powers," groaned the director.

"Ready? Action!"

TELEPROMPTER

DROP THOSE GUNS, YOU ROTTEN ROBBER RATS!

"Cut!" called the director. "Set up for the bionic leap. Wilbur, you pose for three shots. Remember, just look like it's easy. The editor will put these shots together so that it looks like you did it yourself."

"Boy, I'm glad I don't really have to hop up there. High places make me dizzy."

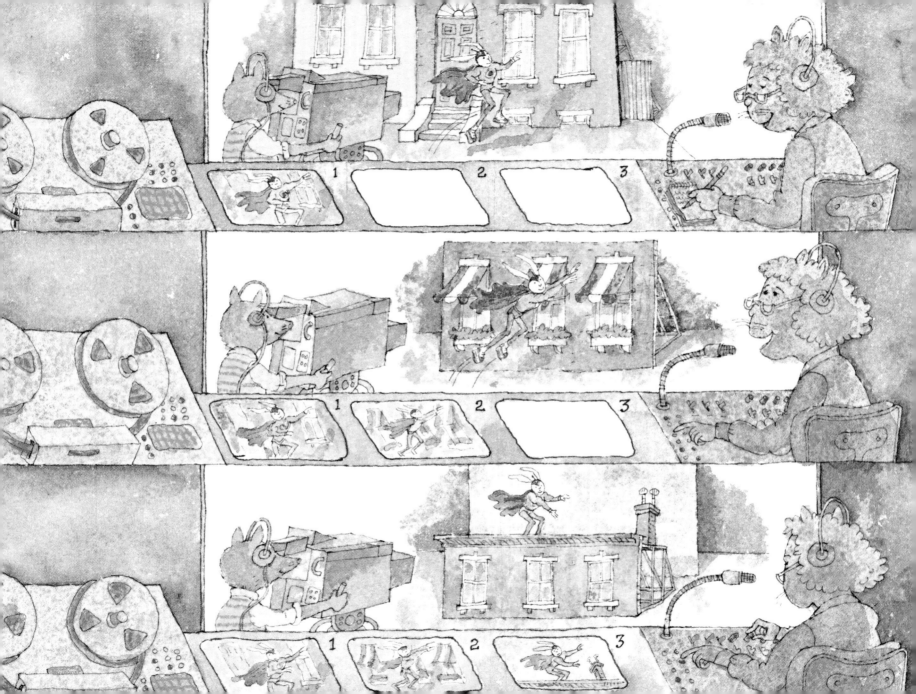

"Cut!" screamed the director.

"Help! I'm drowning!" cried Wilbur. "I can't swim."

"This is supposed to be a storm, not a tornado!" yelled the director.

"Turn down the wind machine. Control room, less thunder and lightning. Prop Department, bring out the giant cat balloons."

"Cut!" announced the director. "Another show finished. Good work, cast. Wilbur, make sure you know your lines better tomorrow when the Bionic Bunny meets the giant green gerbils from Mars."

"You're kidding," groaned Wilbur.

Wilbur said a tired goodnight to the cast and went to his dressing room. Here he slipped off his bionic sneakers, pulled off his bionic ears and wristwatcher, carefully hung up his costume with the built-in muscles, and headed home.

"Hello, dear," said his wife. "You're just in time to help with dinner. Can you open this jar?"

"Just twitch your nose, Daddy," suggested the twins.

"And wiggle your ears," giggled the triplets.

"Look!" cried the triplets. "Bubba opened the jar! And he didn't even twitch his nose or wiggle his ears."

Television Words and What They Mean

*The starred (*) words are all in the story.
See if you can find them.*

actor: a person whose job is to play the part of a character on a t.v. show

*cast: all of the actors who work on a t.v. show

*control room: a separate room that overlooks the television studio. Here the director, sound and lighting engineers, and script person check the show on t.v. screens, making any corrections that are needed

*costume: clothes an actor wears to look like the character he is playing in a t.v. show

*director: the person who is in charge of all of the people working on a show

editing: the process of choosing and putting together smoothly the best pieces of film or videotape in order to make the show you see on your screen

*props: (short for "properties") all the objects, large and small, used by actors in a t.v. show

script: a typed story that tells the characters in a t.v. show what to say and do

*set: painted scenery and props designed to look like the places where the show is said to be happening

superhero: a character who seems to be able to do things real people can't actually do

special effects: using cameras, lights, other equipment, and editing to make something look different; often, the impossible is made to seem real

*teleprompter: a machine that shows an actor his lines in case he should forget them

television studio: a room with t.v. cameras, special lights, and other equipment used in making t.v. shows